Gropp

SOUNDS OF SILENCE

POEMS AND SONGS ABOUT LONELINESS
SELECTED BY BETSY RYAN

✓ S0-CPQ-439

SCHOLASTIC BOOK SERVICES
New York Toronto London Auckland Sydney Tokyo

For reprint permission, grateful acknowledgement is made to:

Cheval-Stanyan Company for "Empty Is" by Rod McKuen from the book IN SOMEONE'S SHADOW, published by Cheval Books. Copyright © 1968 by Editions Chanson Company.

Alan Dugan for "Tribute to Kafka for Someone Taken" from COLLECTED POEMS, © Copyright 1961, Alan Dugan. First published by Yale University Press.

Elsevier Publishing Company, Amsterdam, The Netherlands, for William Faulkner's "Acceptance Speech" for the Nobel Prize reprinted from THE NOBEL PRIZE LIBRARY, pages 7 & 8.

Faber and Faber Ltd. for Canadian rights to "The Hollow Men" by T. S. Eliot from COLLECTED POEMS and "The Unknown Citizen" by W. H. Auden from COLLECTED SHORTER POEMS 1927-1957.

Grove Press, Inc. for "Unwanted" by Edward Field from STAND UP, FRIEND, WITH ME. Copyright © 1963 by Edward Field.

Harcourt Brace Jovanovich, Inc. for "the Cambridge ladies who live in furnished souls" by E. E. Cummings from his volume, POEMS 1923-1954, copyright 1923, 1951 by E. E. Cummings; "Confession Overheard in a Subway" by Kenneth Fearing from AFTERNOON OF A PAWNBROKER AND OTHER POEMS, copyright, 1943, by Kenneth Fearing; renewed 1970, by Bruce Fearing; "The Hollow Men" by T. S. Eliot from COLLECTED POEMS 1909-1962, copyright, 1936, by Harcourt Brace Jovanovich, Inc., copyright © 1963, 1964 by T. S. Eliot.

Harper & Row Publishers, Inc. for "At the Aquarium" by Max Eastman from POEMS OF FIVE DECADES. Copyright 1954 by Max Eastman.

Holt, Rinehart and Winston, Inc. for "Acquainted with the Night" by Robert Frost from THE POETRY OF ROBERT FROST, edited by Edward Connery Latham, copyright 1928, © 1969 by Holt, Rinehart and Winston, Inc., copyright © 1956 by Robert Frost; "Evening" by A. Lutsky, translated by Meyer Liben from A TREASURY OF YIDDISH POETRY edited by Irving Howe and Eliezer Greenberg, copyright © 1969 by Irving Howe and Eliezer Greenberg.

The Macmillan Company for "I Shall Not Care" by Sara Teasdale from COLLECTED POEMS, copyright 1915 by The Macmillan Company, renewed 1943 by Mamie T. Wheless; "An Irish Airman Foresees His Death" by William Butler Yeats from COLLECTED POEMS, copyright 1919 by The Macmillan Company, renewed 1947 by Bertha Georgie Yeats.

The Macmillan Company of Canada for Canadian rights to "An Irish Airman Foresees His Death" by William Butler Yeats from THE COLLECTED POEMS of W. B. Yeats.

New Directions Publishing Corporation for "In A Station of the Metro" by Ezra Pound from PERSONAE, copyright 1926 by Ezra Pound.

Paulist/Newman Press for "Shells Upon the Shore" from DISCOVERY.

Random House, Inc. for an excerpt from the Prologue to INVISIBLE MAN by Ralph Ellison, copyright 1952 by Ralph Ellison; "The Unknown Citizen" by W. H. Auden from the THE COLLECTED POETRY OF W. H. AUDEN, copyright 1940 and renewed 1968 by W. H. Auden.

Scholastic Magazines, Inc. for "every interested friend's duty" by Linda Bauder, "Fences" by Pamela Dean, "Grandfather" by Jean Itzin, "To Talk to You" by Jean Itzin, "Truck Drivers" by Terri Haag, copyright © 1971 by Scholastic Magazines, Inc.

G. T. Sassoon, Heytesbury House, Wiltshire, England, for "Alone I Hear the Wind About My Walls" by Siegfried Sassoon from THE HEART'S JOURNEY.

Sheed & Ward, Inc., New York for a hymn by Gertrud Von Le Fort from HYMNS TO THE CHURCH.

Twayne Publishers, Inc. for "Outcast" by Claude McKay from SE-
LECTED POEMS OF CLAUDE McKAY, copyright 1953.
Wesleyan University Press for "The Missing Person" by Donald
Justice from NIGHT LIGHT, copyright © 1966 by Donald Justice.
The poem was first published in THE NEW YORKER.

PHOTO CREDITS

Jeremiah Bean: 15, 16, 18, 22, 31, 32-33, 43, 60, 68, 79, 84, 88-89; Robert
Burrough: 55; John Gruen: 59; Richard Hutchings: 21, 24, 25, 29, 47,
55, 64-65, 66, 74, 75, 76, 82, 86, 90, 91, 93; Walter Jackson: 9, 63; Ellen
Kattelle: 26, 34-35; Dale Moyer: 13, 44; Greg Wozney: 72.

1st printing ....February 1972
Printed in the U.S.A.

CONTENTS

SONGS

POEMS

PROSE

QUOTATIONS

He was alone. He was unheeded. He was alone and young and willful and wild-hearted, alone amidst a waste of wild air and veiled grey sunlight.

James Joyce
Portrait of the Artist as a Young Man

He is one of those who has had the wilderness for a pillow, and called a star his brother. Alone. But loneliness can be a communion.

Dag Hammarskjold
Markings

. . . ever and forever I am only in myself. I can find no rest in my many chambers, the stillest of them is like a single cry.

Gertrud Von Le Fort
Hymns to the Church

ELEANOR RIGBY

Ah, look at all the lonely people!
Ah, look at all the lonely people!

Eleanor Rigby picks up the rice in the
    church where a wedding has been,
  Lives in a dream.
Waits at the window, wearing the face that
    she keeps in a jar by the door,
  Who is it for?

All the lonely people, where do they all
    come from?
All the lonely people, where do they all
    belong?

Father McKenzie, writing the words of a
    sermon that no one will hear.
  No one comes near.
Look at him working, darning his socks in
    the night when there's nobody there,
  What does he care?

All the lonely people, where do they all
    come from?
All the lonely people, where do they all
    belong?

Eleanor Rigby died in the church and was
buried along with her name,
Nobody came.
Father McKenzie, wiping the dirt from his
hands as he walks from the grave,
No one was saved.

All the lonely people, where do they all
come from?
All the lonely people, where do they all
belong?

John Lennon and Paul McCartney

AN IRISH AIRMAN FORESEES
HIS DEATH

I know that I shall meet my fate
Somewhere among the clouds above;
Those that I fight I do not hate,
Those that I guard I do not love;
My country is Kiltartan Cross,
My countrymen Kiltartan's poor,
No likely end could bring them loss
Or leave them happier than before.
Nor law, nor duty bade me fight,
Nor public men, nor cheering crowds,
A lonely impulse of delight
Drove to this tumult in the clouds;
I balanced all, brought all to mind,
The years to come seemed waste of breath,
A waste of breath the years behind
In balance with this life, this death.

W. B. Yeats

ALONE

"*When I'm alone*"—the words tripped off
  his tongue
As though to be alone were nothing strange.
"*When I was young,*" he said; "*when I was
  young. . . .*"

I thought of age, and loneliness, and change.
I thought how strange we grow when we're
  alone,
And how unlike the selves that meet and
  talk,
And blow the candles out, and say good
  night.
Alone. . . . The word is life endured and
  known.
It is the stillness where our spirits walk
And all but inmost faith is overthrown.

Siegfried Sassoon

11

NOWHERE MAN

He's a real Nowhere Man,
Sitting in his Nowhere Land,
Making all his nowhere plans for nobody.
Doesn't have a point of view;
Knows not where he's going to.
Isn't he a bit like you and me?

Nowhere Man, please listen,
You don't know what you're missing,
Nowhere Man. The world is at your
    command.

He's as blind as he can be;
Just sees what he wants to see.
Nowhere Man, can you see me at all?
Doesn't have a point of view;
Knows not where he's going to.
Isn't he a bit like you and me?

Nowhere Man, don't worry.
Take your time; don't hurry.
Leave it all till somebody else lends you
    a hand.

He's a real Nowhere Man,
Sitting in his Nowhere Land,
Making all his nowhere plans for nobody,
Making all his nowhere plans for nobody,
Making all his nowhere plans for nobody.

John Lennon and Paul McCartney

Alive but alone—belonging where?

W. H. Auden
"Age of Anxiety"

Which of us has known his brother?
Which of us has looked into his father's
heart . . . which of us is not forever a
stranger and alone?

Thomas Wolfe
Look Homeward, Angel

THE MISSING PERSON

He has come to report himself
A missing person.

The authorities
Hand him the forms.

He knows how they have waited
With the learned patience of barbers

In small shops, idle,
Stropping their razors.

But now that these spaces in his life
Stare up at him blankly,

Waiting to be filled in,
He does not know how to begin.

Afraid
That he may not answer even

To his description of himself,
He asks for a mirror.

They reassure him
That he can be nowhere

But wherever he finds himself
From moment to moment,

Which, for the moment, is here.
And he might like to believe them.

But in the mirror
He sees what is missing.

It is himself
He sees there emerging

Slowly, as from the dark
Of a furnished room.

Only by dark,
One who receives no mail

And is known to the landlady only
For keeping himself to himself,

And for whom it will be years yet
Before he can trust to the light

This last disguise, himself.

Donald Justice

SHELLS UPON THE SHORE

"Is it raining outside?" George asks as he sits by his desk in the office. His hellos and goodbyes flood the hours 9 thru 5. There was a time when George would talk about what really mattered to him, but no one seemed to be listening. His words were lost amid financial statements from department #72.

George rides home by train to his split-level outside the city. "Yes, dear, it's been a busy day," he answers Martha. After dinner he lies down on the couch and takes it straight from Huntley and Brinkley. Around ten their daughter Kathy rushes in, slamming the door behind her. "What happened?" they ask. "You wouldn't understand," she mutters, but she sees in their eyes they did not hear her. "Nothing, nothing at all," she sighs as she starts up the stairs.

SHE'S LEAVING HOME

Wednesday morning at five o'clock as the
    day begins
Silently closing her bedroom door
Leaving the note that she hoped would say
    more
She goes downstairs to the kitchen clutching
    her handkerchief
Quietly turning the backdoor key
Stepping outside she is free.
She (We gave her most of our lives)
is leaving (Sacrificed most of our lives)
home (We gave her everything money could
    buy)
She's leaving home after living alone
For so many years. Bye, Bye

Father snores as his wife gets into her
    dressing gown
Picks up the letter that's lying there
Standing alone at the top of the stairs
She breaks down and cries to her husband
Daddy our baby's gone.
Why would she treat us so thoughtlessly
How could she do this to me.
She (We never thought of ourselves)
is leaving (Never a thought for ourselves)
home (We struggled hard all our lives to
    get by)
She's leaving home after living alone
For so many years. Bye, Bye
Friday morning at nine o'clock she is far
    away
Waiting to keep the appointment she made
Meeting a man from the motor trade.
She (What did we do that was wrong)
is having (We didn't know it was wrong)
fun (Fun is the one thing that money can't
    buy)
Something inside that was always denied
For so many years. Bye, Bye
She's leaving home bye bye.

John Lennon and Paul McCartney

I THINK IT'S GOING TO RAIN TODAY

Broken windows and empty hallways
A pale dead moon in a sky streaked with
    gray
Human kindness is overflowing and I
Think it's going to rain today

Scarecrows dressed in the latest styles with
Frozen smiles to chase love away
Human kindness is overflowing and I
Think it's going to rain today

Lonely— — — — — —
Lonely— — — — — —
Tin can at my feet think I'll kick
It down the street
That's the way to treat a friend

Bright before me the signs implore me
"Help the needy and show them the way"
Human kindness why it's overflowing and I
Think it's going to rain today

Randy Newman

SOLEMN HOUR

Who weeps now anywhere in the world,
senselessly weeps in the world,
weeps for me.

Who laughs now anywhere in the night,
senselessly laughs in the night,
laughs me down.

Who walks now anywhere in the world,
senselessly walks in the world,
walks my way.

Who dies now anywhere in the world,
senselessly dies in the world,
sees my face.

Rainer Maria Rilke
(translated by Niel Glixon)

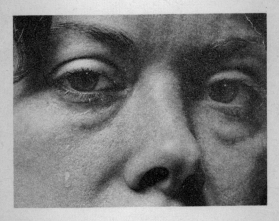

every interested friend's duty

   i've
left him so
pat me on the back
   convince me
i'm right
i have told you all
   fill me
again with words
—i still know, don't i,
how to touch—

   hold
my shoulders they're
shaking
   with laughter
convince me
i've left him
   —pat me right
together—
glue me with kisses
everybody loves a loser.

                    Linda Bauder

UNWANTED

The poster with my picture on it
Is hanging on the bulletin board in the Post
    Office.

I stand by it hoping to be recognized
Posing first full face and then profile.

But everybody passes by and I have to admit
The photograph was taken some years ago.

I was unwanted then and I'm unwanted now
Ah guess ah'll go up echo mountain and crah.

I wish someone would find my fingerprints
    somewhere
Maybe on a corpse and say, You're it.

Description: Male, or reasonably so
White, but not lily-white and usually deep-red

Thirty-fivish, and looks it lately
Five-feet-nine and one-hundred-thirty pounds:
    no physique

Black hair going gray, hairline receding fast
What used to be curly, now fuzzy

Brown eyes starey under beetling brow
Mole on chin, probably will become a wen

It is perfectly obvious that he was not
        popular at school
No good at baseball, and wet his bed.

His aliases tell his history: Dumbbell,
        Good-for-nothing,
Jewboy, Fieldinsky, Skinny, Fierce Face,
        Greaseball, Sissy.

Warning: This man is not dangerous, answers
        to any name
Responds to love, don't call him or he will
        come.

Edward Field

LET ME COME IN

Darkness comes down now, hardly can see,
I feel a darkness rising in me.
Out on the outside, that's where I've been.
Out on the outside, let me come in.

Look through the window, give me some
   light,
Tell me you love me. Say it's all right.
Open the door now, I lost my key.
Shut out the darkness rising in me.

I keep on knocking, no one is there.
Windows are black and the walls are all bare.
I stand in the darkness, followed by fear,
Tell me I'm dreaming, tell me you're here.

Look through the window, give me some
   light,
Tell me I'm home now, say it's all right.
Out on the outside, that's where I've been.
Mother and father, let me come in.

Will Holt

Why are the times so dark
Men know each other not at all,
But governments quite clearly change
From bad to worse?
Days dead and gone were more worth while,
Now what holds sway? Deep gloom and
   boredom,
Justice and law nowhere to be found.
I know no more where I belong.

Eustache Deschamps
15th century

ISN'T IT A PITY?

Isn't It A Pity;
Now, isn't it a shame,
how we break each other's hearts
and cause each other pain.
How we take each other's love
without thinking any more;
Forgetting to give back;
Isn't It A Pity?
Some things take so long,
but, how do I explain,
when not too many people
can see we're all the same.
And because of all their tears
their eyes can't hope to see
the beauty that surrounds them.
Isn't It A Pity?
Forgetting to give back;
Now, Isn't It A Pity?

George Harrison

ACQUAINTED WITH THE NIGHT

I have been one acquainted with the night.
I have walked out in rain—and back in rain.
I have outwalked the furthest city light.

I have looked down the saddest city lane.
I have passed by the watchman on his beat
And dropped my eyes, unwilling to explain.

I have stood still and stopped the sound of
  feet
When far away an interrupted cry
Came over houses from another street,

But not to call me back or say good-by;
And further still at an unearthly height
One luminary clock against the sky

Proclaimed the time was neither wrong nor
  right.
I have been one acquainted with the night.

Robert Frost

OUTCAST

For the dim regions whence my fathers came
My spirit, bondaged by the body, longs.

Words felt, but never heard, my lips would
    frame;
My soul would sing forgotten jungle songs.
I would go back to darkness and to peace,
But the great western world holds me in fee,
And I may never hope for full release
While to its alien gods I bend my knee.
Something in me is lost, forever lost,
Some vital thing has gone out of my heart,
And I must walk the way of life a ghost
Among the sons of earth, a thing apart.

For I was born, far from my native clime,
Under the white man's menace, out of time.

Claude McKay

STRANGER'S BLUES

I'm a stranger here, just blowed in your
    town;
I'm a stranger here, just blowed in your
    town;
Just because I'm a stranger, everybody wants
    to run me around.

I'm a stranger here, please don't drive me
    away;
I'm a stranger here, please don't drive me
    away;
'Cause I might turn out to be your very best
    friend someday.

Well I wonder does my good man know I'm
    here;
Well, I wonder does my good man know I'm
    here;
Well if he does, you know he just don't seem
    to care.

I'm gonna write my momma, send me my
    railroad fare;
I'm gonna write my momma, tell her send
    me my railroad fare;
If it don't come soon, well you know, I don't
    mind walking there.

Well I'm going back home if I wear out all
    my shoes;
Well I'm going back home if I wear out all
    my shoes;
'Cause when I get there, I won't have to
    have those old stranger blues.

I'm a stranger here, stranger everywhere;
I'm a stranger here, stranger everywhere;
Well, I would go home, but you know,
    honey, I'm a stranger there.

I'm a stranger there.

Words and Music by "Tampa Red" Hudson Whittaker.

INVISIBLE MAN

I am an invisible man. No, I am not a spook like those who haunted Edgar Allan Poe; nor am I one of your Hollywood-movie ectoplasms. I am a man of substance, of flesh and bone, fiber and liquids—and I might even be said to possess a mind. I am invisible, understand, simply because people refuse to see me. Like the bodiless heads you see sometimes in circus sideshows, it is as though I have been surrounded by mirrors of hard, distorting glass. When they approach me they see only my surroundings, themselves, or figments of their imagination— indeed, everything and anything except me.

Ralph Ellison

I'm nobody! Who are you?
Are you nobody too?

Emily Dickinson
"I'm Nobody"

THE HOLLOW MEN

Mistah Kurtz—he dead.

A penny for the Old Guy

I

We are the hollow men
We are the stuffed men
Leaning together
Headpiece filled with straw. Alas!
Our dried voices, when
We whisper together
Are quiet and meaningless
As wind in dry grass
Or rats' feet over broken glass
In our dry cellar

Shape without form, shade without colour,
Paralysed force, gesture without motion;

Those who have crossed
With direct eyes, to death's other Kingdom
Remember us—if at all—not as lost
Violent souls, but only
As the hollow men
The stuffed men.

II

Eyes I dare not meet in dreams
In death's dream kingdom
These do not appear:

There, the eyes are
Sunlight on a broken column
There, is a tree swinging
And voices are
In the wind's singing
More distant and more solemn
Than a fading star.

Let me be no nearer
In death's dream kingdom
Let me also wear
Such deliberate disguises
Rat's coat, crowskin, crossed staves
In a field
Behaving as the wind behaves
No nearer—

Not that final meeting
In the twilight kingdom

III

This is the dead land
This is cactus land
Here the stone images
Are raised, here they receive
The supplication of a dead man's hand
Under the twinkle of a fading star.

Is it like this
In death's other kingdom
Waking alone
At the hour when we are

Trembling with tenderness
Lips that would kiss
Form prayers to broken stone.

IV

The eyes are not here
There are no eyes here
In this valley of dying stars
In this hollow valley
This broken jaw of our lost kingdoms

In this last of meeting places
We grope together
And avoid speech
Gathered on this beach of the tumid river

Sightless, unless
The eyes reappear
As the perpetual star
Multifoliate rose
Of death's twilight kingdom
The hope only
Of empty men.

V

Here we go round the prickly pear
Prickly pear prickly pear
Here we go round the prickly pear
At five o'clock in the morning.

Between the idea
And the reality

Between the motion
And the act
Falls the Shadow
     For Thine is the Kingdom

Between the conception
And the creation
Between the emotion
And the response
Falls the Shadow
      Life is very long

Between the desire
And the spasm
Between the potency
And the existence
Between the essence
And the descent
Falls the Shadow
     For Thine is the Kingdom

For Thine is
Life is
For Thine is the

This is the way the world ends
This is the way the world ends
This is the way the world ends
Not with a bang but a whimper.

       T. S. Eliot

CONFESSION OVERHEARD IN A SUBWAY

You will ask how I came to be
    eavesdropping, in the first place.
The answer is, I was not.
The man who confessed to these several
    crimes (call him John Doe) spoke into my
    right ear on a crowded subway train,
    while the man whom he addressed (call
    him Richard Roe) stood at my left.
Thus, I stood between them, and they talked,
    or sometimes shouted, quite literally
    straight through me.
How could I help but overhear?
Perhaps I might have moved away to some
    other strap.
But the aisles were full.
Besides, I felt, for some reason, curious.

"I do not deny my guilt," said John Doe.
    "My own, first, and after that my guilty
    knowledge of still further guilt.
I have counterfeited often, and successfully.
I have been guilty of ignorance, and talking
    with conviction. Of intolerable wisdom,
    and keeping silent.

Through carelessness, or cowardice, I have
    shortened the lives of better men. And the
    name for that is murder.
All my life I have been a receiver of stolen
    goods."
"Personally, I always mind my own
    business," said Richard Roe. "Sensible
    people don't get into those scrapes."

I was not the only one who overheard this
    confession.
Several businessmen, bound for home, and
    housewives and mechanics, were within
    easy earshot.
A policeman sitting in front of us did not
    lift his eyes, at the mention of murder,
    from his paper.
Why should I be the one to report these
    crimes?
You will understand why this letter to your
    paper is anonymous. I will sign it:
    Public-spirited Citizen, and hope that it
    cannot be traced.

Kenneth Fearing

LITTLE BOXES

Little boxes, on the hillside,
Little boxes, made of ticky-tacky,
Little boxes, little boxes, little boxes, all the
   same.
There's a green one and a pink one and a
   blue one and a yellow one,
And they're all made out of ticky-tacky and
   they all look just the same.

And the people in the houses all go to the
   University,
Where they all get put in boxes, little boxes,
   all the same,
And there's doctors and there's lawyers and
   business executives,
And they're all made out of ticky-tacky and
   they all look just the same.

And they all play on the golf-course and
   drink their martinis dry,
And they all have pretty children and the
   children go to school.
And the children go to summer camp and
   then to the University,
And they all get put in boxes and they all
   come out the same.

And the boys go into business and marry
and raise a family,
And they all get put in boxes, little boxes,
all the same.
There's a green one, and a pink one, and a
blue one, and a yellow one,
And they're all made out of ticky-tacky and
they all look just the same.

Malvina Reynolds

TO TALK TO YOU

the words
I want to say
fall cringing
to the floor,
scurrying into corners
seeking shadows,
hiding from your gaze.

Jean Itzin

HOW I FEEL

Hard to tell you how I feel
Everything is so unreal
Lord, but life is a hard thing to get to.

Saw my shadow on the wall
Saw my love nowhere at all
Saw my life as a hard thing to get through.

When you're born they carry you
When you're gone they bury you
In between you're on your own
Hard to stand there all alone.

Someone's crying down the hall
Dying cries they tell it all
Lord, this life is a hard thing to live
And harder still to leave.

Will Holt

SORRY—GRATEFUL

You're always sorry, you're always grateful,
You're always wond'ring what might have
    been,
Then she walks in.
And still you're sorry, and still you're
    grateful,
And still you wonder, and still you doubt,
    and she goes out.
Ev'ry-thing's diff'rent, nothing's changed,
Only maybe slightly rearranged.
You're sorry—grateful, regretful—happy,
Why look for answers where none occur?
You always are what you always were,
Which has nothing to do with,
All to do with her.

You're always sorry, you're always grateful,
You hold her, thinking, "I'm not alone."
You're still alone.
You don't live for her, you do live with her.
You're scared she's starting to drift away,
    and scared she'll stay.
Good things get better, bad get worse.
Wait, I think I meant that in reverse.
You're sorry—grateful, regretful—happy,
Why look for answers where none occur?
You'll always be what you always were,
Which has nothing to do with,
All to do with her.

                                    Stephen Sondheim

ME AND BOBBY McGEE

Busted flat in Baton Rouge; headin' for the
    trains,
Feelin' nearly faded as my jeans;
Bobby thumbed a diesel down just before it
    rained;
Took us all the way to New Orleans.
I took my harpoon out of my dirty, red
    bandanna
And was blowing sad, while Bobby sang
    the blues;
With them windshield wipers slappin' time
    and Bobby clappin' hands,
We fin'ly sang up ev'ry song that driver
    knew.

Freedom's just another word for nothin' left
    to lose,
And nothin' ain't worth nothin', but it's
    free;
Feeling good was easy, Lord, when Bobby
    sang the blues;
And, buddy, that was good enough for me;
Good enough for me and Bobby McGee.

From the coal mines of Kentucky to the
  California sun,
Bobby shared the secrets of my soul;
Standin' right beside me, Lord, through
  everything I done,
And every night she kept me from the cold.
Then somewhere near Salinas, Lord, I let
  her slip away,
Lookin' for the home I hope she'll find;
And I'd trade off all my tomorrows for a
  single yesterday,
Holdin' Bobby's body next to mine.

Freedom's just another word for nothin' left
  to lose,
And nothin' left is all she left for me;
Feeling good was easy, Lord, when Bobby
  sang the blues;
And, buddy, that was good enough for me;
Good enough for me and Bobby McGee.

Kris Kristofferson and Fred Foster

NO LOVE AT ALL

I see in the paper nearly ev'ry day,
people breakin' up and just walkin' away
   from love,
and that's wrong, that's so wrong.
A happy little home comes up for sale
because two fools have tried and failed
to get along,
and you know that's wrong.
A man hurts a woman and a woman hurts
   a man
and neither one of them wanna love and
   understand,
and take it with a grain of salt.
But I believe that a little bit of love
is better than no love,
Even a sad love is better than no love,
Even a bad love is better than no love at
   all.
I got to believe that a little bit of love
is better than no love,
Even a sad love is better than no love,
Any kind of love is better than no love at
   all.
No love at all is a poor old man
standin' on the corner with his hat in his
   hand
and no place to go, he's feelin' low.
No love at all is a child in the street,
dodgin' traffic and beggin' to eat
on the tenement row,
and that's a tough row to hoe.

No love at all is a troubled young girl
standin' on a bridge, on the edge of
  the world,
and it's a pretty short fall.
But I believe that a little bit of love
is better than no love,
Even a sad love is better than no love,
Even a bad love is better than no love
  at all.
I got to believe that a little bit of love
is better than no love,
Even a sad love is better than no love,
Any kind of love is better than no love
  at all.
March out with love to the beat of the
  drum,
Give out your love, got to give it to
  someone.
Spread a little joy, spread a little sunshine.
Give a little kindness, spread a little
  goodness,
Come on people, now, try it one time.
'Cause I believe that a little bit of love
is better than no love,
Even a sad love is better than no love,
Even a bad love is better than no love at all.
I got to believe that a little bit of love
is better than no love,
Even a sad love is better than no love,
Any kind of love is better than no love
  at all.

Words and music by Wayne Carson Thompson
and Johnny Christopher

WHAT HAVE THEY DONE
TO MY SONG, MA?

Look what they done to my song, ma,
Look what they done to my song.
Well it's the only thing
That I could do half-right
And it's turning out all wrong, ma,
Look what they done to my song.
Look what they done to my brain, ma,
Look what they done to my brain.
Well they picked it like a chicken bone
And I think I'm half insane, ma,
Look what they done to my song.
Wish I could find a good book to live in,
Wish I could find a good book to live in.
Well if I could find a real good book
I'd never have to come out and look at
What they done to my song.

Look what they done to my song.
But maybe it'll be all right, ma,
Maybe it'll all be okay.
Well if the people are buying tears
I'll be rich someday, ma,
Look what they done to my song.
Ils ont changé ma chanson, ma,
Ils ont changé ma chanson.
Look what they done to my song, ma,
Look what they done to my song.
Well they tied it up in a plastic bag
And turned it upside down, ma,
Look what they done to my song.
C'est la seule chose que je peux faire,
Et ce n'est pas bon, ma.
Ils ont changé ma chanson.
Look what they done to my song, ma,
Look what they done to my song.
It's the only thing I could do all right
And they turned it upside down.
Oh ma,
Look what they done to my song.

Melanie Safka

LET'S GET TOGETHER

Love is but the song we sing and fear's the
   way we die.
You can make the mountains ring or make
   the angels cry,
Know the dove is on the wing and you need
   not know why.

C'mon, people, now, smile on your brother.
Let's get together, try to love one another
Right now.

Some will come and some will go, and we
   shall surely pass
When the one who left us here returns for
   us at last.
We are but a moment's sunlight, fading on
   the grass.

C'mon, people, now, smile on your brother.
Let's get together, try to love one another
Right now.

If you heard the song I sing, you must
   understand
You hold the key to love and fear all in your
   trembling hand.
One key unlocks them both, you know, and
   it's at your command.

C'mon, people, now, smile on your brother.
Let's get together, try to love one another
Right now.

Love is but the song we sing and fear's the
  way we die.
You can make the mountains ring or make
  the angels cry,
Know the dove is on the wing and you need
  not know why.

C'mon, people, now, smile on your brother.
Let's get together, try to love one another
Right now.

Words and music by Chet Powers

WHO CAN I TURN TO
When Nobody Needs Me?

Who can I turn to when nobody needs me?
My heart wants to know and so I must go
  where destiny leads me.
With no star to guide me, and no one
  beside me,
I'll go on my way, and after the day,
The darkness will hide me.
And maybe tomorrow I'll find what I'm after
I'll throw off my sorrow, beg, steal or borrow
  my share of laughter.
With you I could learn to, with you on a new
  day,
But who can I turn to if you turn away?

Words and music by Leslie Bricusse and
Anthony Newley

Don't ever tell anybody anything. If you do, you start missing everybody.

J. D. Salinger
The Catcher in the Rye

TRUCK DRIVERS

At two a.m.,
the sad-eyed conquerors sit
hunched in familiar
leatherette booths,
waiting for the weariness
to pass,
waiting to be on their roads again.
Their honky music
hangs in the air
like yesterday's cigar smoke,
and the songs are about
themselves.
They talk together
like long-time companions,
knowing they may never
meet again,
and knowing it doesn't matter.
They've met themselves
a million times
in a million roadside,
run-down cafes,
drank countless cups of
black, bitter coffee,
talked countless conquests
of roads and women.
The stories are all the same,
and only the faces
have been changed.
Men of the black mainstreams
of America,

you know this land
from smoky, sprawling city
to silent two-house towns,
you know this land.
Crossing, recrossing the night highways,
delivering America's
abundance,
you've learned the maps
by heart.
Sad-eyed conquerors,
drink your coffee,
think of home.

Terri Haag

DON'T THINK TWICE, IT'S
ALL RIGHT

Well, it ain't no use to sit and wonder why
   babe—
If you don't know by now.
Well, it ain't no use to sit and wonder why
   babe—
It don't matter anyhow.

When the rooster crows at the break of dawn,
Look out your window and I'll be gone.
You're the reason I'm traveling on,
But don't think twice, it's all right.

And it ain't no use in turning on your light,
   babe—
A light I never know.
And it ain't no use in turning on your light—
I'm on the dark side of the road.

Still I wish there was something you could
   do or say
Make me want to change my mind and stay.
We never did too much talking anyway.
Don't think twice, it's all right.

And it ain't no use in calling out my name,
   babe—
Like you never did before.
And it ain't no use in calling out my name—
I can't hear you anymore.

I'm thinking and wondering all the way
   down the road,
I once loved a woman, a child, I'm told.
I gave her my heart, she wanted my soul,
But don't think twice, it's all right.

And I'm going down that long, lonesome
   road, babe—
Where I'm bound I can't tell.
But goodbye is too good a word—
So I'll just say, fare thee well.

I ain't saying you treated me unkind,
Could've done better, but I don't mind.
You just kind of wasted my precious time.
But don't think twice, it's all right.

                              Bob Dylan

... she asked me if I loved her. I said
that sort of question had no meaning
really; but I supposed I didn't.

Albert Camus
The Stranger

TRIBUTE TO KAFKA FOR SOMEONE TAKEN

The party is going strong.
The doorbell rings. It's
for someone named me.
I'm coming. I take
a last drink, a last
puff on a cigarette,
a last kiss at a girl,
and step into the hall,

bang,

shutting out the laughter. "Is
your name you?" "Yes."
"Well come along then."
"See here. See here. See here."

Alan Dugan

WITHIN YOU, WITHOUT YOU

We were talking—about the space between
   us all
And the people—who hide themselves
   behind a wall of illusion
Never glimpse the truth—then it's far too
   late—when they pass away.

We were talking—about the love we all
   could share—when we find it
To try our best to hold it there—with our
   love
With our love—we could save the world
   —if they only knew.
Try to realize it's all within yourself
   no one else can make you change
And to see you're really only very small,
and life flows on within you and
   without you.

We were talking—about the love that's
gone so cold and the people
who gain the world and lose their soul—
they don't know—they can't see—are
    you one of them?
When you've seen beyond yourself—
then you may find, peace of mind is
    waiting there—
And the time will come when you see
We're all one, and life flows on
    within you and without you.

George Harrison

I AM A CHILD IN THESE HILLS

I am a child in these hills
I am away, I am alone
I am a child in these hills
And looking for water
And looking for water.

Who will show me the river
And ask me my name
There's nobody near me to do that
I have come to these hills
I will come to the river
As I choose to be gone
From the house of my father
I am a child in these hills
I am a child in these hills.

Chased from the gates of the city
By no one who touched me
I am away, I am alone
I am a child in these hills
And looking for water
And looking for life.

Who will show me the river
And ask me my name
There's nobody near me to do that
I have come to these hills
I will come to the river
As I choose to be gone
From the house of my father
I am a child in these hills
I am a child in these hills.

Jackson Browne

WHAT KIND OF FOOL AM I?

What kind of fool am I who never fell
   in love?
It seems that I'm the only one that I have
   been thinking of.
What kind of man is this? An empty shell,
A lonely cell in which an empty heart
   must dwell.
What kind of lips are these that lied with
   every kiss?
That whispered empty words of love that
   left me alone like this.
Why can't I fall in love like any other man?
And maybe then I'll know what kind of
   fool I am.

What kind of fool am I who never fell
   in love?
It seems that I'm the only one that I have
   been thinking of.
What kind of man is this? An empty shell,
A lonely cell in which an empty heart
   must dwell.
What kind of clown am I? What do I know
   of life?
Why can't I cast away the mask of play
   and live my life?
Why can't I fall in love like other people can?
And maybe then I'll know what kind of
   fool I am.

Music and lyrics by Leslie Bricusse and
Anthony Newley

From the musical production STOP THE WORLD—I WANT TO
GET OFF. © Copyright 1961 Essex Music, Ltd., London, England.
TRO-Ludlow Music, Inc., New York, N.Y., controls all publication
rights for the U.S.A. and Canada. Used by permission.

THE UNKNOWN CITIZEN

(To JS/07/M/378 This Marble Monument Is
    Erected by the State)

He was found by the Bureau of Statistics to
    be
One against whom there was no official
    complaint,
And all the reports on his conduct agree
That, in the modern sense of an old-
    fashioned word, he was a saint,
For in everything he did he served the
    Greater Community.
Except for the War, till the day he retired
He worked in a factory and never got fired,
But satisfied his employers, Fudge Motors
    Inc.
Yet he wasn't a scab or odd in his views,
For his Union reports that he paid his dues,
(Our report on his Union shows it was
    sound)
And our Social Psychology workers found
That he was popular with his mates and
    liked a drink.
The Press are convinced that he bought a
    paper every day
And that his reactions to advertisements were
    normal in every way.
Policies taken out in his name prove that he
    was fully insured,

And his Health-card shows he was once in
    hospital but left it cured.
Both Producers Research and High-Grade
    Living declare
He was fully sensible to the advantages of
    the Installment Plan
And had everything necessary to the
    Modern Man,
A phonograph, a radio, a car and a frigidaire.
Our researchers into Public Opinion are
    content
That he held the proper opinions for the
    time of year;
When there was peace, he was for peace;
    when there was war, he went.
He was married and added five children
    to the population,
Which our Eugenist says was the right
    number for a parent of his generation,
And our teachers report that he never inter-
    fered with their education.
Was he free? Was he happy? The question is
    absurd:
Had anything been wrong, we should
    certainly have heard.

W. H. Auden

RICHARD CORY

Whenever Richard Cory went down town,
  We people on the pavement looked at him:
He was a gentleman from sole to crown,
  Clean favored, and imperially slim.

And he was always quietly arrayed,
  And he was always human when he
    talked;
But still he fluttered pulses when he said,
  "Good-morning," and he glittered when
    he walked.

And he was rich—yes, richer than a king—
  And admirably schooled in every grace:
In fine, we thought that he was everything
  To make us wish that we were in his place.

So on we worked, and waited for the light,
  And went without the meat, and cursed
    the bread;
And Richard Cory, one calm summer night,
  Went home and put a bullet through his
    head.

Edwin Arlington Robinson

the Cambridge ladies

the Cambridge ladies who live in furnished
    souls
are unbeautiful and have comfortable minds
(also, with the church's protestant blessings
daughters, unscented shapeless spirited)
they believe in Christ and Longfellow, both
    dead,
are invariably interested in so many things—
at the present writing one still finds
delighted fingers knitting for the is it Poles?
perhaps. While permanent faces coyly bandy
scandal of Mrs. N and Professor D
. . . . the Cambridge ladies do not care, above
Cambridge if sometimes in its box of
sky lavender and cornerless, the
moon rattles like a fragment of angry candy

e e cummings

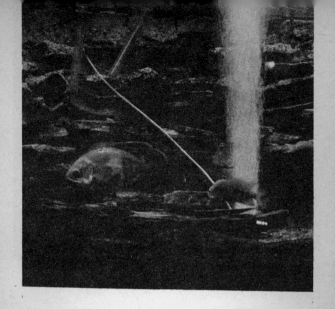

AT THE AQUARIUM

Serene the silver fishes glide,
Stern-lipped, and pale, and wonder-eyed!
As through the aged deeps of ocean,
They glide with wan and wavy motion!
They have no pathway where they go.
They flow like water to and fro.
They watch with never-winking eyes,
They watch with staring, cold surprise,
The level people in the air,
The people peering, peering there:
Who also wander to and fro,
And know not why or where they go,
Yet have a wonder in their eyes,
Sometimes a pale and cold surprise.

Max Eastman

EVENING

Do you think only you are sad and lonely
  at evening time?
All things on the lonely earth
Become lonely in the evening.

Look at the staring houses,

The frightened signs,

The very twigs under your feet.

The blades of grass tremble like small
  children
In the dark fields.

Even the whirr of the far-off wagons
At the boundaries of the world . . .

Can you hear?

A. Lutzky

I'm lonely—
I'll make me a world.

James Weldon Johnson
"The Creation"

WALK A MILE IN MY SHOES

If I could be you and you could be me
    for just one hour,
If we could find a way to get inside each
    other's mind,
If you could see me through your eyes
    instead of your ego,
I believe you'd be surprised to see that
    you'd been blind.

Now your whole world you see around you
    is just a reflection,
And the law of common says you reap
    just what you sow.
So unless you've lived a life of total per-
    fection,
You'd better be careful of every stone that
    you throw.

And yet we spend the day throwing stones
    at one another,
Cause I don't think or wear my hair the
    same way you do.
Well I may be common people, but I'm
    your brother,
And when you strike out and try to hurt
    me, it's a hurtin' you.

There are people on reservations and out
   in the ghettos;
And, brother, there but for the grace of
   God, go you and I.
If I only had the wings of a little angel,
Don't you know I'd fly to the top of the
   mountain.
And then I'd cry.

Walk a mile in my shoes, walk a mile
   in my shoes.
And before you abuse, criticize and accuse,
Walk a mile in my shoes.

Joe South

GRANDFATHER

grandfather glares
madly
through the foggy
vicissitudes
of the minor characters
in his dime-store drama,
his life
a mask, a shadow,
a disguise,
a joke on Aunt Martha
who ponders infinitely
over what to serve
for dinner,
the pretense lives
on through the evening
until the joke
becomes stale,
when grandfather stops
rocking
and wonders casually
when he will be allowed
to die.

Jean Itzin

LONELINESS

I was about to go, and said so;
And I had almost started for the door.
But he was all alone in the sugar-house,
And more lonely than he'd ever been before.

We'd talked for half an hour, almost,
About the price of sugar, and how I like
    my school,
And he had made me drink some syrup hot,
Telling me it was better that way than when
    cool.

And I agreed, and thanked him for it,
And said good-bye, and was about to go.
Want to see where I was born?
He asked me quickly. How to say no?

The sugar-house looked over miles of valley.
He pointed with a sticky finger to a patch
    of snow
Where he was born. The house, he said,
    was gone.
I can understand these people better,
    now I know.

Brooks Jenkins

The apparition of these faces in the crowd;
Petals on a wet, black bough.

Ezra Pound
"In a Station of the Metro"

THERE BUT FOR FORTUNE

Show me the prison, show me the jail
Show me the prisoner whose life has
  gone stale
And I'll show you, young man, with so
  many reasons why
That there but for fortune go you or I.

Show me the alley, show me the train
Show me the hobo who sleeps out in
  the rain
And I'll show you, young man, with so
  many reasons why
That there but for fortune go you or I.

Show me the whiskey stains on the floor
Show me the drunkard as he stumbles out
  the door
And I'll show you, young man, with so
  many reasons why
That there but for fortune go you or I.

Show me the country where the bombs
  had to fall
Show me the ruins of the buildings once
  so tall
And I'll show you, young man, with so
  many reasons why
That there but for fortune go you or I.

Phil Ochs

FENCES

Across the rumbling bus the sign proclaims
that We Sell Fence
                         chainlinked
                         iron
                         barriers

linemarks, boundaries, separations
and they make the spaces in between
the links exactly
> just too
> small
to fit a hand through.
And how cleverly they
> make the faces
> on the other side
> distorted,
> picture-puzzled,
> ugly.
Fence. An ugly word, somewhat,
unless you stare at it long enough
between the letters, and steal it
> of its meaning.
Fence and fennel, rosemary and basil.
Gather it by moonlight.
Again, an ancient wizard's name:
> And Fence came unto the land
> and lifting up his hand he
> cried aloud and shook the stones.
And fence again, to keep dogs out and
people in and
> tell the world what's whose.
> Iron fence, it says.
One trusts most carefully
> in rust.

Pamela Dean

We glide past each other. But why? Why?
We reach out towards the other in
vain—because we have never dared to
give ourselves.

Dag Hammarskjold
Markings

FOR EVERYWHERE ON EARTH

For everywhere on earth blows the wind of
  forsakenness, hark, how it moans over
  the spaces of the world!
Everywhere there is one and never two.
Everywhere is a cry in a prison and a hand
  behind locked doors;
Everywhere there is one buried alive.
Our mothers weep and our beloved are
  speechless; for none can help the other:
  each and all are alone.
They call to one another from silence to
  silence, they kiss one another from
  solitude to solitude. They love one another
  a thousand griefs away from their souls.
For the nearness of men is like flowers
  withering on graves, and all comfort is
  like a voice from without—
But you are a voice in the inmost soul.

Gertrud Von Le Fort

THE CITY

The restless and noisy activity of the
crowded streets is highly distasteful, and it
is surely abhorrent to human nature itself.
Hundreds of thousands of men and women
drawn from all classes and ranks of society
pack the streets of London. Are they not
all human beings with the same innate
characteristics and potentialities? And do
they not all aim at happiness by following
similar methods? Yet they rush past each
other as if they had nothing in common.
They are tacitly agreed on one thing
only—that everyone should keep to the
right of the pavement so as not to collide
with the stream of people moving in the
opposite direction. No one even thinks of
sparing a glance for his neighbors in the
streets. The more that Londoners are packed

into a tiny space, the more repulsive and
disgraceful becomes the brutal indifference
with which they ignore their neighbors and
selfishly concentrate upon their private
affairs. We know well enough that this
isolation of the individual—this
narrow-minded egotism—is everywhere the
fundamental principle of modern society.
But nowhere is this selfish egotism so
blatantly evident as in the frantic bustle of
the great city. The disintegration of society
into individuals, each guided by his private
principles and each pursuing his own aims,
has been pushed to its furthest limits in
London. Here indeed human society has
been split into its component atoms.

Friedrich Engels, writing in 1844.

EMPTY IS

Empty is
the sky before the sun wakes up the morning.
The eyes of animals in cages.
> The faces of women mourning
> when everything has been taken
> > from them.

Me?
> Don't ask me about empty.

Rod McKuen

I SHALL NOT CARE

When I am dead and over me bright April
   Shakes out her rain-drenched hair,
Though you should lean above me
     broken-hearted,
  I shall not care.

I shall have peace, as leafy trees are peaceful
   When rain bends down the bough;
And I shall be more silent and cold-hearted
   Than you are now.

Sara Teasdale

Speech is civilization itself—it is
silence which isolates.

Thomas Mann
The Magic Mountain

EVERYBODY'S TALKIN'

Everbody's talk'n at me
I don't hear a word they're say'n
Only the echoes of my mind

People stop'n star'n
I can't see their faces
Only the shadows of their eyes

I'm go'n where the sun keeps shin'n
Through the pour'n rain
Go'n where the weather suits my clothes
Begg'n off of the northeast winds
Sail'n on the summer breeze
Skipp'n over the ocean like a storm

Everybody's talk'n at me
Can't hear a word they're say'n
Only the echoes of my mind
I won't let you leave my love behind
I won't let you leave my love behind

Fred Neal

ACCEPTANCE SPEECH

I feel that this award was not made to me as a man, but to my work—a life's work in the agony and sweat of the human spirit, not for glory and least of all for profit, but to create out of the materials of the human spirit something which did not exist before. So this award is only mine in trust. It will not be difficult to find a dedication for the money part of it commensurate with the purpose and significance of its origin. But I would like to do the same with the acclaim too, by using this moment as a pinnacle from which I might be listened to by the young men and women already dedicated to the same anguish and travail, among whom is already that one who will some day stand here where I am standing.

Our tragedy today is a general and universal physical fear so long sustained by now that we can even bear it. There are no longer problems of the spirit. There is only the question: When will I be blown up? Because of this, the young man or woman writing today has forgotten the problems of the human heart in conflict with itself which alone can make good writing because only that is worth writing about, worth the agony and the sweat.

He must learn them again. He must teach himself that the basest of all things

is to be afraid; and, teaching himself that,
forget it forever, leaving no room in his
workshop for anything but the old verities
and truths of the heart, the old universal
truths lacking which any story is ephemeral
and doomed—love and honor and pity
and pride and compassion and sacrifice.
Until he does so, he labors under a curse.
He writes not of love but of lust, of
defeats in which nobody loses anything of
value, of victories without hope and,
worst of all, without pity or compassion.
His griefs grieve on no universal bones,
leaving no scars. He writes not of the heart
but of the glands.

Until he relearns these things, he will
write as though he stood among and
watched the end of man. I decline to accept
the end of man. It is easy enough to say that
man is immortal simply because he will
endure: that when the last dingdong of
doom has clanged and faded from the last
worthless rock hanging tideless in the last
red and dying evening, that even then
there will still be one more sound: that
of his puny inexhaustible voice, still
talking. I refuse to accept this. I believe
that man will not merely endure: he will
prevail. He is immortal, not because he
alone among creatures has an inexhaustible

voice, but because he has a soul, a spirit capable of compassion and sacrifice and endurance. The poet's, the writer's, duty is to write about these things. It is his privilege to help man endure by lifting his heart, by reminding him of the courage and honor and hope and pride and compassion and pity and sacrifice which have been the glory of his past. The poet's voice need not merely be the record of man, it can be one of the props, the pillars to help him endure and prevail.

William Faulkner